EVERY FRIDAY

DAN YACCARINO

SQUARE
FISH

Henry Holt and Company
New York

SQUARE
FISH
An Imprint of Macmillan

Library of Congress Cataloging-in-Publication Data
Yaccarino, Dan.
p.   cm.
Summary: Every Friday a father and his child share a special ritual.

ISBN 978-1-250-00473-4

[1. Father and child—Fiction. 2. City and town life—Fiction.] I. Title.
PZ7.Y125Eve2006   [E]—dc22   2005020253

Originally published in the United States by Henry Holt and Company
First Square Fish Edition: May 2012
Square Fish logo designed by Filomena Tuosto
Book designed by Dan Yaccarino and Donna Mark
The artist used gouache on watercolor to create the illustrations for this book.
mackids.com

10 9 8 7 6 5 4 3 2 1

AR: 1.4

AUTHOR'S NOTE

Every Friday, my son, Michael, and I have breakfast together
at the corner diner. Since he turned three, this has been
our special time together and our favorite day of the week.
I hope that you, too, will start a little tradition like ours.

Friday is my favorite day.

Every Friday, Dad and I leave the house early.

Even if it is cold,

snowing,

sunny,

or raining.

We see the shops open.

And the building on the corner going up bit by bit.

We look at lots of things along the way.

"Three more blocks to go," says Dad.

Everyone is rushing, but we're taking our time.

We get friendly waves,

and we give them right back.

We count the dogs,

and I mail our letters with a little help.

"C'mon," I say.

"Only one more block to go."

At last—breakfast at the diner!

"Let me guess," Rosa the waitress says.
"Pancakes, right?"

We look out the window
and watch people hurry by.

While we eat, Dad and I talk about

all sorts of things.

But soon it's time for us to go.

Already, I can't wait.